BAKER & TAYLOR

W9-BXD-136

STARTING HOME

STARTING HOME

THE STORY OF HORACE PIPPIN, PAINTER

MARY E. LYONS

CHARLES SCRIBNER'S SONS • NEW YORK
Maxwell Macmillan Canada • Toronto
Maxwell Macmillan International
New York • Oxford • Singapore • Sydney

ACKNOWLEDGMENTS

I am grateful to the following people and institutions for their help in locating information on Horace Pippin: Judith Stein of the Pennsylvania Academy of Fine Arts; Eulie Costello of the Goshen, New York, Public Library; Gertrude and John Bruen of Goshen, New York; The Chester County Historical Society; The Archives of American Art, Smithsonian Institution; The National Archives; and Mrs. Alice Carlen.

Additional information was found in:

Rodman, Selden. *Horace Pippin: A Negro Painter in America.* New York: The Quadrangle Press, 1947.
———. *Horace Pippin: The Artist as a Black American.* New York: Doubleday & Co., 1972.

I am especially grateful to the National Endowment for the Humanities and the DeWitt Wallace Reader's Digest Fund. Their generous Teacher-Scholar Award provided the time and financial support necessary to research the life of Horace Pippin.

Charles Scribner's Sons Books for Young Readers
Macmillan Publishing Company
866 Third Avenue, New York, NY 10022

Maxwell Macmillan Canada, Inc.
1200 Eglinton Avenue East, Suite 200
Don Mills, Ontario M3C 3N1

Macmillan Publishing Company is part of the Maxwell Communication Group of Companies.

First edition   10 9 8 7 6 5 4 3 2 1
Printed in Hong Kong
Book design by Vikki Sheatsley

Library of Congress Cataloging-in-Publication Data
Lyons, Mary (Mary E.)
    Starting home : the story of Horace Pippin, painter / Mary E. Lyons.
        p.   cm.
    Summary: Discusses the life and work of the African-American folk artist Horace Pippin.
    ISBN 0-684-19534-8
1. Pippin, Horace, 1888–1946—Juvenile literature. 2. Afro-American painters—Biography—Juvenile literature. [1. Pippin, Horace, 1888–1946. 2. Artists. 3. Afro-Americans—Biography. 4. Painting, American. 5. Painting, Modern—20th century. 6. Art appreciation.] I. Title.
ND237.P65L86 1993   759.13—dc20   [B]   92-26990

To David Kherdian

Horace painted his first version of this scene in 1935. He often painted the same subject three or four times. "Cabin in the Cotton III," 1944. Oil on canvas. 23 × 29¼. Collection of Mr. Roy R. Neuberger, New York City. Photograph by Geoffrey Clements.

• ONE •

Horace Pippin's pencil had a mind of its own. Every time the teacher called out a spelling word, his pencil drew a picture. "Dog," she said. D-O-G wrote Horace on his paper. And a picture of a dog appeared right after the letter *G*.

"Stove," his teacher called. S-T-O-V-E Horace spelled. Before he could stop the pencil, it drew a stove. Horace didn't know what to do.

"Dishpan," she announced. D-I-S-H-P-A-N, and there was a picture of a dishpan. Horace decided he was in trouble. He was right. The teacher made him stay after school and do his lesson over. He was only seven, but he had to sit in the one-room school house on Merry Green Hill after everybody else was gone. And he knew the worst was yet to come.

Horace dragged his feet in the dirt road as he walked the three blocks home. By the time he reached the railroad tracks that ran beside his house, he was moving as slow as a slug. Horace was late again, and a whipping would be waiting for him.

After he had grown up and become a famous painter, Horace remembered that his pencil always got him into trouble. "This happened frequently," he wrote, "and I just couldn't help it."

One day ten-year-old Horace saw a contest advertised in a magazine. There was a picture of a funny face. "MAKE ME," said large letters under the face, "and win a prize." Horace drew the picture and sent it to Chicago. The next week a package arrived in the mail. He had won the prize: a box of paint, two brushes, and six colored pencils.

He cut six circles out of muslin fabric and fringed the edges. Using his new pencils, he drew a scene from the Bible in the center of each circle. When his Sunday school held a festival, Horace hung the homemade doilies on the wall to be sold. After an elderly lady bought them all, he was so excited that he ran home to share the good news with his mother.

But a week later, the lady stopped Horace on his way to school. "Are you Horace Pippin?" she called. She sounded as if she had fish bones in her mouth.

Horace nodded.

Her mouth shriveled up. "Did you make them six tickies?" she asked. Horace had good manners and a friendly smile. He decided to use them both now.

"Yes, ma'am," he said, and grinned at her.

"You certainly make some bum things," the woman said, spitting out the words. She pulled a clean piece of fringed muslin out from under her apron. "Look at this. I bought it at the festival with a picture on it. I washed it and this is all I have!"

He tried to explain that a penciled picture could not be washed. But he knew from the look on her face that it was no use. Horace Pippin and his pencil were in trouble again.

Over forty years later, he still remembered how the lady had washed his artwork away. The memory was so strong that he painted doilies over and over, sometimes placing them on armchairs, often on a table. Even the fringe that Horace made reappears in many of his pictures.

Horace had deep feelings about other events and places in his life. These, too, found their way into his drawings and paintings. Like a scrapbook, each piece of art reveals a piece of his past. "Pictures just come to my mind," he once said, "and then I tell my heart to go ahead."

Horace Pippin was born in 1888 in West Chester, Pennsylvania, but he had no childhood memories of West Chester. When he was three, his parents moved with him and his younger brother, John, to Goshen, New York. Goshen was called the land of milk, cream, and butter because there were so many dairy farms in the area.

Little is known about Horace's father, Daniel Pippin. He worked as a laborer and died when Horace was ten. Horace's mother worked as a cleaning woman in private

The two chairs and pictures give this scene perfect balance. The painting was named by art dealer Robert Carlen. *"Victorian Interior,"* 1945. *Oil on canvas. 25¼ × 30. The Metropolitan Museum of Art, New York City. Arthur Hoppock Hearn Fund, 1958.*

A letter from the Goshen Public Library inspired Horace to paint this scene from his childhood. A year later he wrote to the library, "Then I painted 'The Milk Man of Goshen,' so you see I think you gave me the idea of it." *"The Milkman of Goshen,"* 1945. Oil on canvas. 31 × 25. *Private Collection, Philadelphia, Pennsylvania. Courtesy of Sotheby's, Inc., New York.*

homes and was a well respected member of her community.

Shortly after Daniel died, Christine Pippin married a man named Green. They had four daughters, and the family lived at 339 West Main Street, a few blocks from the center of town. African Americans had settled in two sections of Goshen. "Up on Green" was a wetland area near a pond on the edge of town. Here the poorest black people lived in dirt-floor shacks where they sank up to their ankles in mud on rainy days. Horace and his family lived "Over the Hill," a better neighborhood, where black Civil War veterans had bought homes with their pensions.

Their two-story house sat on a large lot. The generous grassy lawn was big enough for cider parties and croquet games with the neighborhood children. And there was plenty of space left for his mother to raise her beloved roses.

Horace's painting "The Milkman of Goshen" shows small-town life at the turn of the twentieth century. The building in the painting once stood across the street from Horace's home. It was called a double-house, and like many buildings of the time, it had a tin roof. The stacked wood and sawhorse tell us that the homes were heated with wood. The rain barrel collected water for cooking and drinking.

Each morning the milkman brought fresh milk to sell from his wagon. The women, wearing fringed shawls, waited while he filled their small pails. Perhaps the little girl was one of Horace's younger sisters.

Christine read the Bible to her children and told them stories about her mother, who had been a slave in Virginia. Horace heard how his grandmother watched the hanging of John Brown. The story became so real to him that he later painted three pictures of John Brown. Horace's grandmother appears in "John Brown Going to His Hanging."

John Brown was an antislavery leader who wanted to free all the slaves. He planned to establish a hideaway in the mountains for them. Guns were needed for the operation, so he and a group of men tried to capture the United States arsenal of weapons at Harpers Ferry, Virginia (now West Virginia). Brown was wounded in the raid and went to trial on a stretcher. On December 2, 1859, he was hanged at what is now Charles Town, West Virginia.

Looking at the painting, it's easy to feel

the gloom of that December day. A few forlorn leaves hang from the trees. John Brown, tied with rope, sits on his own coffin.

Horace's grandmother stares from a corner of the canvas. He has made her easy to see. She is the only black person and the only woman in the picture. Her fringed shawl and bright blue dress stand out against the dark clothes of the men around her. Her face shows the same anger that all slaves felt when they lost their hero, John Brown. The painting is a story, and Horace's grandmother is the teller of the tale.

Years later he painted other pictures of black life remembered from childhood. It's likely that he saw the 1932 film about white sharecroppers *Cabin in the Cotton*. The movie may have reminded him of southern scenes that his mother had described when he was a boy. When Horace painted his own version of the Cabin in the Cotton (shown facing page 1), he sprinkled the picture with reminders of African-American culture and history.

The man and woman are probably sharecroppers, farming someone else's land in exchange for a small part of the harvest. They are poor, and she wears a shirt so ragged that it looks fringed. The kerchief tied around her head is a dress custom that enslaved women brought with them from Africa. She is smoking a pipe. Perhaps it is a clay pipe like the ones that African potters made when they arrived in the New World. The man is playing a banjo, a stringed instrument much like those that his ancestors had played in Africa. Both are wearing red, a color important in African religions.

Horace Pippin is famous for the use of red in his paintings. Red stands out in another scene recalled from his childhood, "Domino Players." This painting shows Horace's memory of a black family in the kitchen. In many turn-of-the-century homes, the kitchen was the center of family life. It was a place to share food and warmth, to play games, to be together.

Horace shows that this, too, was a poor family. The plaster is peeling from the walls. The window shade is worn thin. The center slat of the chair on the left is broken. But the red grate of the coal-burning stove warms the group, and oil lamps brighten the room with spots of ruby light.

Horace tells us through his art that there was little money when he was growing up in

"John Brown's Body" was the unofficial theme song of African-American soldiers in the Civil War: "John Brown's body lies a-mouldering in the grave, / But his soul goes marching on." *"John Brown Going to His Hanging," 1942. Oil on canvas. 24⅛ × 30¼. The Pennsylvania Academy of the Fine Arts, Philadelphia. John Lambert Fund.*

Horace called this "The Domino Game." The clock on the shelf shows his concern with time. Clocks and watches appear in many of his works, and he often referred to his "timepiece" in his war diaries. *"Domino Players,"* 1943. Oil on canvas. 12¾ × 22. The Phillips Collection, Washington, D.C.

Goshen, but that didn't stop him from having fun. He learned to play his mother's organ, and on snowy days he liked to watch horse-drawn sleighs race through the middle of town. He also enjoyed playacting with his brother and sisters in Tom-Thumb weddings. These pretend-ceremonies featured children and were named after the famous 1863 wedding of the circus midget Tom Thumb to Lavinia Warren, a dwarf.

On Sunday mornings Horace heard the old cracked bell in the African Methodist Episcopal Church remind him to go to service. Sunday was also "walking day" and time to visit other families in town. In the summer he might have ridden the trolley to nearby Midway Park to hear band concerts.

Horace certainly played in the creek behind the houses across the street. As any mother would do, Christine Green probably warned her son not to play on the Erie Railroad tracks behind the creek. And like children everywhere, he surely did it anyway.

Like the boy seems to be in "Domino Players," Horace was a contented child, surrounded by people who cared about him. But when he was fourteen, boyhood came to a sudden end for Horace Pippin.

• TWO •

Horace needed work. There were seven mouths to feed, and no one else to earn the money. Mr. Green had left the family, and Christine was sick. Horace had finished only six grades, but he was the oldest. Someone had to provide for his mother, brother, and sisters, so he quit school and worked a string of odd jobs.

He was a stable boy on a farm, hauled sacks of corn for a feed store, then drove a coal wagon. Finally, he settled down as a porter at the St. Elmo Hotel. For the next seven years, Horace and his pencil didn't have much time to draw.

The St. Elmo was one of the busiest spots in town. It was built across the street from the train station. A parade of reporters, businessmen, lawyers, and politicians checked in and out of the hotel every day. When a train left or arrived, there was a flurry of chores to be done. Horace carried the men's bags, shined their shoes, and helped them find comfortable chairs for napping on the long covered porch. He may have arranged their bets on the horses at the Goshen Half-Mile harness track.

With fifty-two rooms the St. Elmo was considered a luxury hotel. *Courtesy of the Goshen, New York, Public Library. Photograph reproduction by Frank Stamski III.*

In the summer the owner of the hotel kept his pet alligators in the fountain at the city park. During the winter months they lived in tanks by the boiler in the hotel cellar. Perhaps it was Horace who fed them their daily meal of bullfrogs!

Goshen's harness racing track was the oldest in the world, and the races attracted the rich and famous. One of these was General Ulysses S. Grant. He visited Goshen before Horace was even born, but the stories that the former head of the Union army told about the Civil War and Abraham Lincoln survived

for years. These tales became part of Goshen folklore, and Horace heard them retold at the St. Elmo.

He later recorded one of the stories in a painting called "Abe Lincoln, the Great Emancipator." Lincoln is wearing his famous stovepipe hat and beard. General Grant watches as the president pardons an infantryman who had fallen asleep while on duty.

This picture shows Horace's great regard for Lincoln. He has given the president the role of savior. The soldier kneels at his feet, while Lincoln lays a kind hand upon his

"Abe Lincoln, the Great Emancipator," 1942. Oil on canvas. 30 × 24. Museum of Modern Art, New York City. Gift of Helen Hooker Roelofs.

Horace Pippin as a young man. *The Estate of Carl Van Vechten, Beinecke Rare Book and Manuscript Library, Yale University.*

shoulder. Just as the Emancipation Proclamation freed the slaves from bondage, Abraham Lincoln is freeing the soldier from a cruel punishment. To Horace, Lincoln was the champion of all people, and he became the subject of four of Horace's paintings.

Christine Green died in 1911. After the death of his mother, twenty-three-year-old Horace decided to move on. He left Goshen to work in New Jersey, and when the United States entered World War I, he joined the all-black New York State 15th National Guard Regiment. It was renamed the 369th Regiment upon acceptance into the United States Army, but the soldiers always called it the "old 15th."

Like many African-American men, Horace was eager to fight for his country. "The good old U.S.A. was in trouble with Germany," Horace wrote in his diary, "and to do our duty to her we had to leave here." But some places in the "good old U.S.A." were not eager to have black men join the troops. When Horace's regiment was sent for training in Spartanburg, South Carolina, the townspeople made it clear that they didn't want black soldiers in town. Even the offer of a jazz concert by two musicians from the regiment could not ease the tension. Insults were exchanged. Fights broke out.

If Horace was bitter about this treatment, he never spoke or wrote of it in public. African-American newspapers were watched closely during World War I for any signs of lack of patriotism. Perhaps Horace knew that it would not be safe to talk openly about racism in the armed services.

But his painting "Mr. Prejudice" tells how he felt about being a black man in a white army. The V stands for *victory*. On one side of the V are black servicemen: an infantryman, aviator, sailor, and machinist. The ghostlike figure on the far left may represent black men wounded in the struggle. They are all sheltered by a black Miss Liberty.

On the other side of the V are white men with the same jobs. They seem to be under the power of the Ku Klux Klan and a hangman with a noose. The V is being split like a piece of wood by the figure Mr. Prejudice. How can there be victory, Horace asks in this painting, when a country keeps its sol-

These soldiers from Goshen were members of the "old 15th," the all-black New York State National Guard Regiment. Horace probably is in this picture but has never been identified. *Courtesy of the Goshen, New York, Public Library. Photograph reproduction by Frank Stamski III.*

"Mr. Prejudice," 1943. Oil on canvas. 18 × 14. Private Collection, Dr. and Mrs. Matthew T. Moore.

diers divided? The faces of the men show a mutual distrust. But the figures of the black sailor and white aviator show hope, too. Each has stretched out a hand to his brother.

After two weeks of trouble in South Carolina, the 369th Regiment was ordered to ship out. With no weapons or training to prepare them for war, they became the first unit of American black soldiers to go overseas. Horace spent Christmas Day, 1917, pitching and rolling across the Atlantic Ocean on a ship bound for Europe. After twenty-four days at sea, the ship finally landed on December 27. "Rocking like a drunken man," Horace and the rest of his regiment stepped unsteadily onto the "troublesome ground" of France.

The French soldiers were thrilled to see the black troops. They had been fighting the Germans for three years and were desperate for help. The German forces had pushed west, deep into France. Now the fighting continued along a line called the western front.

Standing like cattle in boxcars, the men were shipped by train toward the front. The weather was harsh. Horace watched snow swirl around his boxcar as it rattled through the countryside. When the snow stopped, the rain and wind began. Some of the men died of influenza.

One day the regiment marched through a town that had been destroyed by German shells. Horace had never seen a place so much in need. Most of the buildings were destroyed. There was literally nowhere to lie down. Old people were living under sheets hung near the road.

Horace looked at them with sorrow. He remembered the poor black people of Goshen who lived in shacks. He had seen poverty and hard times before, and now he felt great sympathy for the people of this "friendless and helpless" French town. As the wind cut through his overcoat, he shivered. Horace was so cold he didn't know what to do. But he knew he was warmer than these men and women, who had only thin blankets to keep out the icy air.

Despite the cold, the snow, and the rain, the 369th Regiment laid five hundred miles of railroad track inland from the sea to the front lines. They unloaded ships and guarded German prison camps. It was hard labor, and their only relaxation came from listening to concerts by the regimental band or from get-

ting a few hours of rest in the barracks. Years later Horace painted "The Barracks," a portrait of the dreary side of war: boredom.

The bleak scene of four men in their bunks could be set in the day or nighttime. "I didn't know if they had a sun there or not," he said of France. ". . . I have not seen the sun in more than a month." At the bottom of the picture, green moss grows on a post that stands in mud—always the infernal mud. World War I has been called the War of Mud, and Horace Pippin never forgot how it felt to walk, eat, and sleep in mud. Whitish mud appears in most of his war paintings.

One of the men in "The Barracks" is reading a treasured letter from home. After food and sleep, nothing was as important as mail call. Horace recalled that when he got a letter from home he was so glad that he couldn't speak. "It were so short that I read it over and over. . . . I could read it by heart and not miss a word of it." When he felt homesick he would pull it out, read it, then "put it away in its old place again." The letter lived in his pocket for so many weeks that the address on the envelope rubbed off.

Horace Pippin's pencil helped him through his year in France. A series of five-

"The Barracks," 1945. Oil on canvas. 25¼ × 30. The Phillips Collection, Washington, D.C.

cent composition books became his traveling companion. In these diaries he recorded his thoughts and drew hundreds of pictures, for the war "brought out all the art in me," he later said.

He recalled that he had to burn most of the notebooks. Perhaps he couldn't carry them all, or they may have contained drawings of weapons and troop positions that he didn't want the Germans to find. He did manage to save one diary with seven drawings. These are the first surviving pictures by the artist Horace Pippin. They are only simple sketches, but they tell a terrible tale.

• THREE •

"I will say this much," Horace wrote about the front-line trenches. "I say no man can do it again. He may have the will but his body cannot stand it." As Horace shows in his pictures, the men on the front lines suffered unimaginable hardships.

They endured blinding gas attacks, long marches with heavy gear on their backs, and muddy trenches soaked with dripping water.

Horace could wash his hands just by pressing them on the posts that supported the dugout walls. Even a cigarette would not light down in the soggy holes.

And there was no-man's-land: the zone of hell between the two armies, where exploding shells from big guns lit up the night and left gaping holes in the earth. "I could tell a new man every time I seen him," Horace wrote, "for he would duck every time a shell come over. He would be ducking all day long until he would get used to it."

The men depended on each other for strength. "They never fear danger," Horace wrote of his fellow soldiers, "and they always give to one another. If there is one who looks downhearted they would cheer him up some way. . . ."

One night the looey, or lieutenant, asked for volunteers. Everyone offered, but only eight were needed. Jerry, as the Germans were called, had dug a line from their main trench out into no-man's-land. Horace's officers expected a visit from a German patrol that night. At eleven o'clock he and the others would follow the looey into no-man's-land and "see to it that no Germans were to go out or in" the trench.

It was hard going. The barbed wire was thick and tangled. Horace helped his men over, although it was so dark and rainy that they could hardly see each other. From shell hole to shell hole they darted, jumping in for cover from constant machine-gun fire. "The bullets were singing their death song through the air," Horace remembered, "and they would hit the wire and glance off and hum like a bee." By one o'clock in the morning only five men were left, huddled together in one hole.

Horace stuck his head above the shell hole and spotted a single Jerry by the light of his gunfire. Soon they circled the German machine-gun man and closed in on him. The soldier threw up his hands, surrendered, and was taken back to the line. But Horace knew the rest of the enemy patrol was still out there in the dark.

Sketches from Horace Pippin's war diary. *Pippin Papers, Archives of American Art, Smithsonian Institution, Washington, D.C.*

A man in a gas mask in a trench—"The gas were strong."

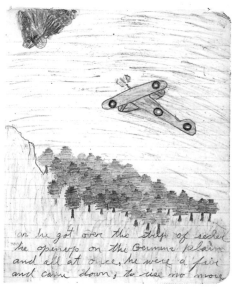

An airplane in the sky—"As he got over the strip of seder he open up on the Germans. . . ."

Three soldiers marching—"I were so cold that I were growing stiff."

The men crawled on their hands and knees with rain running down their rifles like water down a gutter and their clothes soaked through. They "looked with all the eyes they had." Suddenly, "out of the blackness of the night," Horace recalled, "came the sound of an owl. 'Hoo, hoo, hoo.'" The Germans were signaling their man on the machine gun. Horace answered for him.

"Hoo, hoo, hoo," he called back. Soon nine Germans came forward, tricked into capture by the American patrol. But now Horace and his men had to take their dead back through heavy machine-gun fire to the front line. "It were the worst job ever I had," he said later, "to drag a dead man over that rough no-man's-land."

Many of the ingredients of this scene from Horace's diary are present in his painting "Dog Fight Over the Trenches." Two African-American soldiers stand guard over the entrance to the dugout, which is heaped with mud. The borders of no-man's-land are spiked with barbed wire, and blood-red flowers bloom among the shell holes. Leafless stumps and a fallen tree signify the loss of life and limb.

The 369th Regiment spent over six months on the front line without relief. Horace remembered living in the trenches for twenty to thirty days at a time. He was unable to remove any clothing or even his shoes—only his helmet to use as a pillow. Finally, the war came to an end for him in October 1918, just one month before it was declared over throughout Europe.

One morning as he dove for cover in a shell hole, a German sniper shot him in the shoulder with an exploding dumdum bullet. The other four men in the hole tried to bandage his wound, but then had to leave him there. Every time Horace tried to climb out, the sniper fired again. By afternoon, he was too weak to leave on his own.

A French soldier came by and looked down in the hole. Before Horace could warn him, a German bullet passed through the Frenchman's head. "He stood there for at least ten seconds before he slipped down," Horace remembered, "and when he did he slid down on top of me." Horace had lost too much blood to even move the dead man.

By the next day he was rescued from the hole and put on a stretcher, where he lay in the rain all day and night. At last the stretcher-bearers arrived and carried him to

In 1945, twenty-seven years after he was shot, Horace Pippin was awarded a Purple Heart for wounds received in battle. *"Dog Fight Over the Trenches,"* 1935. Hirshhorn Museum and Sculpture Garden, Smithsonian Institution, Washington, D.C. Gift of Joseph H. Hirshhorn, 1966.

a dugout. He waited there for an ambulance to take him to a field hospital. The doctors operated, attaching his shattered right shoulder to his upper arm with a steel plate.

Horace arrived back in the United States by hospital ship on January 5, 1919. He was still recovering in an army hospital when the rest of the 369th Regiment arrived in New York City. He must have been proud when he heard how the men of the "old 15th" marched up Fifth Avenue to Harlem.

Taking short French marching steps, they chose to walk in the same tight formation they had learned from the French. Their French helmets were rusty and dented, and the bayonets on their French rifles were dull. But these African-American soldiers felt honored to have fought alongside the men of France, who had provided them with weapons and welcomed their help without prejudice or question. The 369th was the first American unit to be awarded the highest military medal by the French government: the cross of war, or Croix de Guerre.

Horace couldn't walk in this historic parade. But he had survived. And he had earned the nickname the French gave to all the soldiers of the 369th: Hell Fighters.

• FOUR •

On May 22, 1919, Horace Pippin was discharged from the army with a monthly $22.50 disability pension. Like most men who return from battle, he was a changed man. The war had become a part of him.

The steel plate would remain in his shoulder for the rest of his life. Pain would travel with him wherever he went. And even though Horace had destroyed most of his composition books, the pictures stayed in his head. "I can never forget suffering," he wrote years later, "and I will never forget sunset. That is when you could see [the war]. . . . I came home with all of it in my mind."

There is no battle scene in the picture that Horace painted twenty years after he came home. But "The Getaway" recalls the lonely feelings that sunset brought when he was a soldier. As a wintry moon rises above the trees, a fox heads for home, taking his dead prey with him. The stars of the Little Dipper cast the same cold glow as the stars that Horace saw on long marches through France. Snow covers the barren landscape just as it

"The Getaway," ca. 1939. Oil on canvas. 24 × 35½. Private Collection, Philadelphia, Pennsylvania. Courtesy Janet Fleisher Gallery. Photograph by Norinne Betjemann.

did in war. Horace painted snowy scenes so well that to look at one can almost bring on a chill.

There was no home or job for Horace when he returned to the United States. He didn't know what to do next. He did pay a visit to his half sisters in Goshen. Two of them still lived in the two-story house on West Main Street where they had been born—Sally with her son and daughter, Hattie with her boy. Seeing his niece and nephews play with the neighborhood children in the yard made Horace feel lonesome. He remembered his own peaceful boyhood. But those years had ended when his mother died. Now he had to start a new life.

He visited his brother, John, in New Jersey. A friend there introduced him to the twice-widowed mother of a six-year-old boy. Five-foot Ora Featherstone Wade was as short as Horace was tall, but they were both quiet and kind. Because of his wound, Horace couldn't work. He was a likable man and a gentleman, however, and Ora needed a father for her son. Horace called her Jennie and she called him Pippin. They promised to take care of each other in a marriage ceremony on November 21, 1920.

Jennie's family was from West Chester, Pennsylvania. She wanted to be near her relatives, so the couple moved back to the town where Horace had been born. They lived in a narrow but roomy three-story brick house on Gay Street. Horace would later paint this street in a picture called "West Chester, Pennsylvania."

Although the buildings were crowded together, Gay Street was in a pleasant neighborhood with grassy front yards, hedges, and an occasional picket fence. A large tree grew out of the bumpy brick sidewalk in front of the Pippins' house. Its spreading branches shaded them on hot summer days. The tiny backyard was big enough for a flower garden, roosters and chickens, and a clothesline that was important to their income. Horace's pension was not large enough to live on, so Jennie took in laundry, and he helped her deliver it.

During slavery time, West Chester had been a stop on the Underground Railroad. Pennsylvania was the first free state on the way north, and many former slaves had decided to end their journey to freedom there. But despite the large black population, West Chester was like any other town in the United

A historical marker stands in front of the house on Gay Street where Horace lived from 1920 until 1946. *"West Chester, Pennsylvania," 1942. Oil on canvas. 36 × 29. Wichita Art Museum. The Roland P. Murdock Collection. Photograph by Henry Nelson.*

States: There were few jobs available for African Americans.

If he had been able, Horace could have worked as a janitor or a waiter. There were laborers' jobs in the brickyard and at the wheel works. Some black men worked on the railroad. But except for a few restaurants and a barber shop or two, most businesses were owned and run by white people.

Jennie's son, Richard Wade, attended a segregated school. When they went to the movies, Horace and his family had to sit in the balcony. The YMCA was segregated, as was the football team at the integrated high school.

But Horace and Jennie lived in a racially mixed section of town, and there must have been many moments of friendly warmth and sharing between white and black. He later sketched a scene called "After Supper, West Chester." Two cultures are happily mixed together in the picture. Black and white chil-

"After Supper, West Chester," 1949. Pencil on cardboard. 14 × 22⅛. The Metropolitan Museum of Art, New York City. Bequest of Jane Kendall Gingrich, 1982.

dren are playing a white singing game called, "London Bridge Is Falling Down." An elderly white woman is smoking a clay pipe like the one smoked by the black woman in "Cabin in the Cotton III."

It's no accident that Horace used children to show racial harmony in this sketch. He loved children of all ages. He held Tom-Thumb weddings for Richard and his friends. He helped organize a Boy Scout troop, and neighborhood baseball games were often umpired by Horace. Perhaps he bought a Hokey Pokey, or ice-cream cone, for each kid when the Hokey Pokey wagon slowly rolled by.

The 1920s was a quiet decade for Horace. Despite the pain in his arm, he managed to enjoy life. He and Jennie fished in the Brandywine River, bringing home carp for supper. He went groundhog hunting with friends in nearby Lancaster County. And years later he told a magazine reporter that they always had turkey for Christmas, goose for New Year's, and guinea fowl for birthdays.

Music was important to Horace. He led the drum corps in American Legion parades and sang in the church choir. And despite his limp arm, he managed to play the guitar, mandolin, and organ. In his painting "Harmonizing" Horace. recorded a vital part of African-American music: call and response.

The man on the left is dressed like a preacher. He appears to be the musical leader of the group as he conducts, or calls, the song with his right arm. The other three men follow his lead and respond, or join in with their parts. They may be singing a gospel song or a popular jazz tune they have heard on the radio.

But sometimes the fishing and the hunting and the children and the music were not enough to make the war go away. Horace had only to close his eyes to hear the pounding of shellfire. Twice a month he attended American Legion meetings and shared war stories with other veterans, who called him Pip. But talking and joking about the war did not help him to understand it.

One winter Horace turned to his pencil for help. He decided to write down his memories of World War I. If only he could record what had happened to him, he could finally forget it. Writing was a slow, painful job.

He could move his fingers, but not his arm. With his pencil held tightly in his right

"Harmonizing," 1944. Oil on canvas. 24 × 30. Allen Memorial Art Museum, Oberlin College, Oberlin, Ohio. Gift of Mr. and Mrs. Joseph Bissett, 1964. Color transparency by John Seyfried.

hand, he carefully printed the events of 1917–1918 in neat capital letters. As a guide to help him remember, he read over the only war diary that he had saved from France. He added new information and left some out. But it was no use. "I did such an unsuccessful job I gave it up," he later said of his memoirs.

There was only one way truly to rid himself of the war, and that was impossible because his arm was useless. Horace Pippin's pencil could no longer draw.

• FIVE •

For eleven long years there had been no sketches, no way to put his feelings down on paper. Horace could pick up his pencil. He could write with it by sliding the paper along with his good left hand. But he could not move his pencil around well enough to turn his thoughts into a picture.

One early winter day in 1929, Horace sat near the potbellied stove. He noticed the poker as it rested in the fire. The tip was white-hot. What if . . . ? He grabbed an extra leaf from the golden-oak table and held it up with his strong left arm. Then he laid the handle of the poker in his weak right hand and balanced the poker on his knee.

Horace was eager to begin, for he already had a picture in mind. As he guided the wood behind the poker, he burned lines and curves into the panel. And like a magician, he slowly created the image of a man, a horse, and a wagon. To make the background of dark woods, he pressed evenly into the oak. To draw bare trees, he etched more deeply. To indicate snow, he simply left the light wood as it was.

Horace felt like a genius! His brilliant discovery had set him free. At last he could do what he loved most: draw. The method was tedious, but it worked. He took a year to finish the burnt-wood panel, and when the picture finally suited him he called it "Losing the Way." He neatly burned in the words of the title and proudly signed his name, not with a pencil, but with a poker: HORACE PiPPiN.

Now he longed to paint, for there was another picture that haunted his mind. And perhaps he could hold a paintbrush the same way he held the poker. But where would he get the paint and canvas? The Pippins couldn't afford expensive artists' oils. Horace

Horace continued to make burnt-wood panels for another decade. Many were hunting and fishing scenes set in fall and winter landscapes. *"Losing the Way," 1930. Burnt-wood panel. 12 × 20. The State Museum of Pennsylvania, Harrisburg.*

scavenged the neighborhood for abandoned cans of house paint. He used heavy cotton fabric, or ticking, as a painting surface. A cheap easel held the picture as he worked on it. Jennie may have provided the homemade smock to keep paint from spattering her fastidious husband's white shirt cuffs.

For the next three years, Horace was possessed by one painting. He sat in their "second parlor" and worked under a 200-

watt light bulb. Using tiny brush strokes, he put down a hundred coats of paint trying to make the images look right. This first painting frustrated him, and he later said, "I really couldn't do what I wanted to do." He named the painting "The Ending of the War: Starting Home."

This picture has been called one of the greatest of all war paintings. For Horace it was the beginning of a healing artistic journey. Twelve years after leaving France, he finally was starting home from war. For over a decade he had carried scenes of violence in his head. Like a broken bone that must be reset to mend properly, he had to produce the war again in order to recover from it.

"It came the hard way with me," Horace said of painting about war. Painful memories appeared on the canvas while he worked for as many as seventeen hours at a time. Shellfire exploded, burning airplanes hurtled to the ground, soldiers thrust their bayonets in deadly hand-to-hand combat. He even carved wooden hand grenades, gas masks, and helmets and nailed them to the frame. Not only does Horace Pippin's first painting convey the agony of war, it is also historically accurate.

World War I did not end in victory out in the trenches. It ended inside a warm, dry building hundreds of miles away as all the leaders of the countries involved in the war agreed to a peace treaty. The soldiers were the last to know. As Horace said later in describing "The Ending of the War: Starting Home" to a journalist, he had showed the German soldiers holding up their hands in surrender "because they had to quit before we could go home."

He was entranced by painting. During the 1930s he retreated into the world of his art. "Oh, Horace is painting," the neighbors would say when he wouldn't answer their knock at the door. "We'll come back later." His work was deliberate and thorough. "I take my time and examine every coat of paint carefully. . . ." he said. "When I'm through with a picture, I've put everything in it I've got to give."

In most years he was able to complete two or three paintings. But in some years the pain in his arm kept him from working, and he could only manage one. Visits to the Veterans' Hospital in Philadelphia were not much help.

Jennie liked to see Horace painting be-

"The End of the War: Starting Home," 1931. Oil on canvas. 25 × 32. Philadelphia Museum of Art. Given by Robert Carlen. (Horace Pippin originally called this "The Ending of the War: Starting Home.")

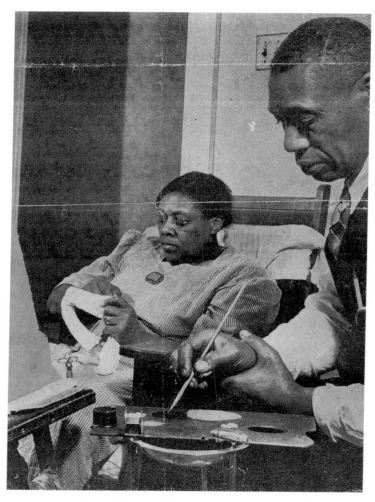

Jennie and Horace Pippin at home. *Photo Archives, Chester County Historical Society, West Chester, Pennsylvania.*

cause she knew it was healthy for his mind *and* his body. Just holding the paintbrush and letting his good arm guide the weak one was enough to make it stronger. Horace knew he was lucky to have Jennie to take care of him. When she fixed his meals, laundered his clothes, and darned his socks, she gave him the gift of time. With Jennie to do these daily and necessary chores, Horace could concentrate on his art.

By 1937 he had completed twenty paintings. He used colors that he called "simple," making sure they were the exact ones he had in mind. The colors were quiet, like Horace—soft greens, faded blues, the muted browns of a military uniform. These early paintings, like the slave spirituals of his ancestors, are dignified but slow and sad. Perhaps that is why his art didn't appeal to the townsfolk of West Chester.

Horace tried to sell his paintings for five dollars. Then he tried to raffle them for one dollar. Finally he tried to give them in payment for bills that he owed. His barber did take a picture in exchange for a haircut, but his wife wouldn't let him hang it. A local black-owned restaurant allowed Horace to display his paintings on the wall. They may have been for sale, but no one was interested in buying Horace Pippin's art.

Horace was forty-nine years old. He had been painting for eight years with no recognition or encouragement, but he would not give up. When he heard that the West Chester County Art Association was having an art show, he entered two paintings. A famous local artist, N. C. Wyeth, saw Horace's pictures of a cabin in the cotton and Abe Lincoln building a log cabin. He thought they were both beautiful. Wyeth suggested to the president of the art association that Pippin deserved a one-man show.

On June 9, 1937, Horace proudly entered the African-American community center in West Chester. He looked with satisfaction at the ten paintings and seven burnt-wood panels hanging on the walls. He was grateful that he didn't have to share the spotlight with someone else. Only works by the artist Horace Pippin were on display.

Wealthy society ladies from Philadelphia attended the exhibit, along with an art critic and an art dealer from New York. Only one painting was sold at Horace's first show, but it was an event that would change the rest of his life.

• SIX •

Two years later a Philadelphia art dealer, Robert Carlen, noticed Horace's paintings at a gallery in New York. He knew he had found a prize artist. Horace agreed to let Carlen sell his paintings, and for the next seven years, the art dealer would be Horace's ally, counselor, even his banker.

Success welcomed Horace like an old friend. In 1940 Carlen held a one-man show for him at the Carlen Gallery in Philadelphia. All twenty-five paintings were sold, five of them to a wealthy Philadelphia art collector named Albert Barnes. Barnes sold "Cabin in the Cotton I" to a Hollywood actor, and soon other actors in California clamored to own a Pippin.

Barnes invited Horace to attend art lectures and view the art collection at his mansion. Barnes figured that since Horace had never studied art it was time that he learned from others. So Horace took the one-dollar train ride from West Chester to the Barnes Foundation every Tuesday.

There was no harm in looking at another painter's pictures, thought Horace, for "his way may help you find your own." But he also believed that "you don't copy him, because what you want to put down is something inside of you and not in anybody else." He enjoyed looking at other paintings, especially those by French painters. "I like them by Renoir," remarked Horace, "because they're full of sunlight." He was already a genius with black, gray, and white, but after seeing how other painters used color, he added bright yellows and rich greens to his palette.

However, he found the lectures boring. He tried to pay attention, but he couldn't help falling asleep. One member of the class remembered that Horace smelled like whiskey. If Horace was drinking in the middle of the day, it is likely that he had been abusing alcohol for some time. He may have started drinking when he was in the army, or perhaps he began using liquor after the war to ease the pain in his arm.

After just two lectures, Horace stopped his visits to the foundation. "I learned a lot," he said, "but I'm going my own way." He knew he could trust himself to paint the pictures in his mind. Horace didn't need a teacher—he was already a master.

When Horace finished a painting or two he brought them to Philadelphia, or Carlen came to pick them up. Robert Carlen made money on every Pippin painting that he sold. But without his special help, there might not have been as many Pippin paintings to sell.

The art dealer stretched heavy cotton over flat wooden bars to make canvases for Horace. He bought brushes and ten-dollar tubes of artists' paints with real pigment—yellow ocher, raw umber, zinc white. Together they hunted through antique and junk shops for inexpensive gold frames.

Carlen made sure that everyone knew about Horace's art. He wrote to the black poet Langston Hughes, and sold a picture to Alain Locke, a well-known black writer who later called Horace a "real and rare genius." Carlen knew these men could spread the word about Horace through the African-American community.

It was Carlen who sent a postcard to the West Chester newspapers to tell them of Horace's $300 award for "The Milkman of Goshen." He tried to arrange a Guggenheim Fellowship, an important award for those with proven talent in the arts. An attempt in the early 1940s to get Horace on the cover of *The Saturday Evening Post* did not succeed because Horace was black. "I am not sure we are ready," replied the editor to Carlen's request, "to use Pippin on our covers yet."

Carlen also helped Horace with research. When Horace was ready to paint the "John Brown" series, Carlen took him to the library. Together they looked through books for pictures of tables, benches, and chairs so that the paintings would be historically accurate.

Even after he became famous, Horace did not desert Carlen. When another art dealer sent a young black man with the message that she could sell more of his paintings, Horace refused to accept her offer. "Why should I?" he answered. "I'm satisfied." Sometimes visitors to his home wanted to buy a painting directly from him. He could have made more money that way. But Horace had learned the value of loyalty from his buddies in the "old 15th" Regiment, and the answer was always no.

During the early years of his success, he was usually broke. Critics loved the "singing colors" and "imaginative patterns" of Horace's art, but the pictures sold for only a few hundred dollars each. The income was not steady, and Horace had little experience in

The shriveled arm and stiff fingers show that Horace Pippin was keenly aware of his war injury when he painted this picture of himself. *"Self Portrait," 1941. Oil on canvas mounted on cardboard. 14 × 11. Albright-Knox Art Gallery, Buffalo, New York. Room of Contemporary Art Fund, 1942.*

managing money. He often wrote to Carlen asking, "IS THERE ANEYTHEiNG [anything] IN FOR ME WILL YOU SEND IT TO ME SOON. AND I WILL THANK YOU. FROM—HORACE PIPPIN.

Jennie said that art was an "unstable" way to earn a living. Maybe her husband's new career would fall apart like a house of cards, she thought. She continued to take in laundry, just in case. Besides, Jennie was proud of the good job that she did, and it made her feel needed.

Success changed Horace's quiet home life. Because of his arm injury, he probably could not drive, but he bought a Buick for his stepson that cost him fifty dollars a month in car-loan payments. Within two months Horace wrote Carlen that the car was "broken up." His stepson, Richard Wade, had tipped it over.

The Pippins' social life changed, too. Now they were invited to the homes of wealthy whites who lived near Philadelphia. Horace and Jennie made quite an impression at these parties. One guest recalled that they were "a perfectly delightful couple." He remembered that "Mrs. Pippin was genuine, warm, bright, and full of laughter." Horace, he said, was "a big man with a powerful frame, a massive, very remarkable head . . ."

It was a treat for Horace to meet other artists at these gatherings. Full of life, his eyes lit up as he talked about his work. Once he and another artist stood on a terrace behind the house and watched the distant hills and trees. Horace constantly looked up from their conversation to absorb the lovely view. He had "an extraordinary love of nature" his companion recalled.

Good luck continued to tap Horace on the back. Between 1938 and 1942 there were seven showings of his paintings at galleries and museums from New York to Chicago to San Francisco. He could hardly paint fast enough to keep up with the demand for his work. Instead of painting one picture a year, now he painted one every month.

But fortune had its price. Horace said painting was "harder" for him after his first exhibition at the Carlen Gallery. Now he felt pressured to paint "better and better" pictures. Perhaps the strain to produce added to his drinking problem. By 1945, Robert Carlen remembered, Horace could drink a quart of Scotch whisky in one afternoon.

America's entry into World War II in 1941

troubled Horace. When his stepson went into the service, he felt a mixture of pride and sorrow. Only a veteran of the previous "war to end all wars" could understand the terrible costs of battle.

On a visit to the Carlen home, Horace saw "Peaceable Kingdom," a painting by Edward Hicks, hanging in the living room. "Why don't you try your own idea of it?" Carlen suggested to Horace. Inspired by Hicks's scene of animals in the forest, Horace painted a series of paintings that were his response to war. They stood for all the good and evil he had seen in his life.

Later renamed "The Holy Mountain," this series was first called "The Knowledge of God." When asked to explain, Horace wrote that the Bible "tells us that the knowledge of God shall be as deep upon the earth as the waters are in the sea. . . ." The African Americans hanging from trees on the extreme left of the painting were his "little ghost-like memory" of lynching. "You will see what they did and are still doing in the South," Horace reminded the viewer. The "little crosses" in the center of the picture, he wrote, "tell us of them in the first world war. . . ." Horace wondered if men still had

Horace Pippin painting *"The Woman at Samaria."*
Courtesy Mrs. Alice Carlen.

"Holy Mountain III," 1945. Oil on canvas. 25¼ × 30¼. *Hirshhorn Museum and Sculpture Garden, Smithsonian Institution, Washington, D.C. Gift of Joseph H. Hirshhorn, 1966.*

the knowledge of God, but he felt sure that "there will be peace."

Like many African-American artists, Horace drew strength from his church and religion. He amazed people with his knowledge of scripture. Stories and figures from the Bible were the subjects of several paintings, including Christ, the Crucifixion, and the Woman at Samaria. Horace stated that he painted out of loneliness, but that his talent came from God. When he had trouble painting, he once said, he prayed, and the next morning he had an answer to his problem.

Jennie's health failed during the war years, and Horace may have turned to his religion for help. Their marriage had been weakened by his many trips out of town and his frequent visits to the corner bar to buy rounds of drinks for everyone. When Jennie thought that Horace was seeing another woman, she became severely depressed.

"Im in a Bad way at this time," Horace wrote to Carlen in 1945. "I do not no [know] what I am doeing [doing]. . . . as you no [know] if your helpmate is bad it makes it bad for all. . . ." Jennie began to suffer from delusions. She had conversations with her dead father and believed that her medicine was poisoned. Horace checked her into a mental hospital in March 1946.

He canceled a June trip to Goshen, where the library had displayed photographs of his paintings. Horace wrote to the library on a card that featured his painting "Victory Vase." "I came to great gladness," he said, ". . . to no [know] that my dear friends put them where every one could see them. . . ." He also finished one of his best paintings, "Man on a Bench." The glorious red of the bench contrasts with the somber figure who sits on it. Horace painted his own feelings into the picture. The man's slumped posture, rumpled clothes, and downcast expression reveal an overwhelming sadness.

Alone now in the empty house on Gay Street, Horace began to drink more than ever. One Friday night in July 1946, he stayed at the bar until the early hours of the morning. He enjoyed the company of the other customers. Sitting around the bar reminded him of the barracks during the war, when lonely boys smoked, told stories, and dreamed of home to keep the blues away.

The next day, July 6, his housekeeper became worried. She knew that Horace liked to sleep past noon. But the hours passed with

"Man on a Bench," 1946. Oil on canvas. 13 × 18. Private Collection, Philadelphia, Pennsylvania. *Courtesy Janet Fleisher Gallery. Photograph by Norinne Betjemann.*

no sound from his room. At 3:45 P.M., she tried to wake him. Sometime during the night, Horace's heart had stopped.

He was buried a few yards from the highway in the Chester Grove Cemetery Annex. No town officials from West Chester came to the funeral of their most famous African-American citizen, but some of Horace's friends from the art world were there. Still in the hospital, Jennie Pippin was not told of her husband's death. She passed away two weeks later.

Some say that Horace Pippin had a noble head like that of the painter Picasso. Others say that his paintings look like those by Matisse. Like these famous men, Pippin is known throughout the world, and his paintings now bring high prices: "The Milkman of Goshen" sold for $100,000 in 1988.

Nevertheless, Horace was different from trained artists. Self-taught, he tells the story of his life in his paintings. They have a beautiful simplicity that can only come from a modest soul. He did not finish school,

Horace Pippin's grave at the Chester Grove Cemetery Annex, Chester County, Pennsylvania.

and he wasn't clever with written words. But with pencil, poker, then paintbrush, Horace Pippin was a poet in the language of art.

INDEX
Page numbers for illustrations are in *italics*

"Abe Lincoln, the Great Emancipator," 10–12, *11*
African-American culture, 5–9, 26, 34, 39
"After Supper, West Chester," *25*, 25–26

Barnes, Albert, 33–34
"Barracks, The," 15, *16*
Brown, John, 5–6

"Cabin in the Cotton I," 33
"Cabin in the Cotton III," *vi*, 6
Carlen, Robert, 33–37
colors, Pippin's use of, 6, 32, 34

"Dog Fight Over the Trenches," 19, *20*
"Domino Players," 6, *8*, 9

"End of the War: Starting Home, The," 29–30, *31*

French, the
  and "old 15th" regiment, 14–15, 21

"Getaway, The," 21–23, *22*
Green, Christine Pippin (Horace's mother), 2–5, 9, 12

"Harmonizing," 26, *27*
"Holy Mountain, The," 37–39
"Holy Mountain III, The," *38*

"John Brown Going to His Hanging," 5–6, *7*, 35

"Knowledge of God, The," 37–39

Lincoln, Abraham, 10–12
"Losing the Way," 28, *29*

"Man on a Bench," 39, *40*
"Milkman of Goshen, The," *4*, 5, 34, 41
"Mr. Prejudice," 13–14, *14*
music and Pippin, 26

"old 15th" regiment, 12, *13*, 14–21, 35

Pippin, Horace, *12*, *32*, *35*, *37*
  and alcohol use, 34, 36, 39
  art techniques of, 2, 28–29, 32, 34–35
  birth of, 2
  death of, 39–41
  education of, 1, 9, 33–34
  family of, 2–5, 23
  finances of, 6–9, 23, 35–36

  and Jennie, 23, 32, 39
  jobs of, 9, 23–25
  and music, 26
  recognition of, 32–33, 34–36, 41
  and religion, 5, 39
  and World War I, 12–21, 26–28, 30
Pippin, Ora Featherstone Wade ("Jennie"), 23, 29, 30–32, *32*, 36, 39
  illness and death of, 39, 41

race relations, 12–14, 25–26, 34–35

"Self Portrait," *35*

"Victorian Interior," *3*
"Victory Vase," 39

Wade, Ora Featherstone ("Jennie"), 23
Wade, Richard (Horace's stepson), 25, 26, 36–37
"West Chester, Pennsylvania," *24*
World War I, 12–13, 14–21
  Pippin's drawings of, 17, *18*, 30, *31*